'She is nigh,' hissed the constable's legs.

A large black limousine whooshed up out of nowhere and purred to a halt. An electric window slid down. Gerald could see only darkness. A chauffeur hurried to open the door.

Out slid an arm, bearing a big red snakeskin handbag. Out slid a pair of great red snakeskin shoes with stiletto heels that would rip your floors to shreds.

In the horrible red shoes were the huge feet belonging on the ends of the legs belonging to Romoana Sneedie.

The boos of the crowd died away as she stood before them, smiling.

Gerald hadn't expected to wake up that Saturday morning to find a pelican asleep next to him. And he is even more surprised to discover that this is a bird with a mission – to protect the local duckpond from infamous Romoana Sneedie.

Romoana is powerful, and her plans to build a hideous leisure complex look unstoppable. But then Gerald and the pelican begin a little direct action . . .

Gerald
and the
Pelican

Caroline Pitcher

Illustrated by Paddy Mounter

YEARLING BOOKS

GERALD AND THE PELICAN

A YEARLING BOOK 0 440 863120

First publication in Great Britain

PRINTING HISTORY
Yearling edition published 1993

Text copyright © 1993 by Caroline Pitcher
Illustrations copyright © 1993 by Paddy Mounter

Conditions of Sale

1. This book is sold subject to the condition that it shall not, by way of trade or otherwise, be lent, re-sold, hired out or otherwise circulated without the publisher's prior consent in any form of binding or cover other than that in which it is published and without a similar condition including this condition being imposed on the subsequent purchaser.

2. This book is sold subject to the Standard Conditions of Sale of Net Books and may not be re-sold in the UK below the net price fixed by the publishers for the book.

Set in 14/16pt Linotype Century Schoolbook by
Phoenix Typesetting, Burley-in-Wharfedale, West Yorkshire.

Yearling Books are published by Transworld Publishers Ltd, 61-63 Uxbridge Road, Ealing, London W5 5SA, in Australia by Transworld Publishers (Australia) Pty. Ltd, 15–25 Helles Avenue, Moorebank, NSW 2170, and in New Zealand by Transworld Publishers (N.Z.) Ltd, 3 William Pickering Drive, Albany, Auckland.

Printed and bound in Great Britain by
Cox & Wyman Ltd, Reading, Berks.

GERALD AND THE PELICAN

CHAPTER ONE

One Saturday morning, Gerald woke up with something sharp digging into his neck.

He turned over and saw that there was a pelican asleep next to him. Its

head was on the pillow. It had a long beak with a little hook on the end. The hook must have been resting in the nape of Gerald's neck.

Gerald was sure the pelican had not been there the night before.

The pelican opened its eyes. They were as hard and bright as marbles. It said, 'Good morning, Gerald. I trust you slept well?' It lifted its head to look around, and its beak whizzed past Gerald's ear like an electric carving knife.

'Watch where you're putting that beak!' cried Gerald.

'I beg your pardon,' said the pelican in its small, gruff voice. 'I meant no harm.'

Gerald wasn't so sure about that.

The pelican heaved itself out from under the duvet and stood up on large, webbed feet, swinging its head from side to side on its long, strong neck. Its feathers were grey and on the top of its head was an extra tuft that stood up like petals on a chrysanthemum.

'I will be able to spend the whole day with you, Gerald,' said the pelican. 'And possibly every third Saturday after that.'

'I don't think I can do with a pelican today,' said Gerald.

'I am a very busy bird,' warned the pelican. 'I have a tight schedule. I am a bird with a mission, Gerald.'

'Lucky you,' grumbled Gerald. 'I have to go campaigning with Mum today. *All* day. Saturday is campaigning day and I'm too young to be left on my own, she says. So I have to be dragged along with all the fogey-bogeys. Mega-bore! She says today is crucial, because Romoana Sneedie is on the move.'

The pelican winced as if it had a pouchful of wasps. 'Sneedie . . .' it squawked. 'The name rings like a death-knell through the world of waterbirds.'

'Eh?' said Gerald.

'I'll explain some other time, Gerald. It really is too early in the morning for such dreadful thoughts,' shuddered the pelican.

'Oh,' said Gerald. 'Anyway, I want to read the rest of *Treasure Island* this evening. You wouldn't like that.'

'On the contrary!' cried the pelican. 'I adore *Treasure Island*. Captain Flint, the parrot, is a fascinating character, don't you agree?'

'How can a bird know about a book?' puzzled Gerald.

'I am not just any old pigeon pulled off the streets, Gerald,' it squawked. 'I am a Crested Pelican. Sometimes I am known as a Dalmatian Pelican. And what is more, I am Perchbird of the Waterbirds' Ponds and Pools Committee . . . I say, I do like your curtains.'

Gerald's bedroom curtains were blue, with an underwater scene of fish and frogmen.

'I like that poster, too – that one of "Fish of the North Sea". I can see we have much in common, Gerald.' The pelican hummed a little tune deep in its pouch. The tune sounded similar to 'Life on the Ocean Waves'.

Suddenly it stopped humming and stared hard at the shelves in the corner. Its head was tilted so that Gerald could see only one fixed eye.

'What's the matter?' he said.

The pelican did not reply. It stretched up on to the very tips of its big webbed feet and ran heavily on the spot.

'Mind my duvet!' cried Gerald, noticing the four sharp claws on each foot. He watched in horror as the bird's head began to swing from side to side and its wings began to flap so that Gerald's hair lifted in the breeze.

He suddenly realized what the pelican was doing. It was preparing for take-off. It was gaining speed, ready to launch itself through the air at the two fat goldfish in their tank on the shelf.

Gerald grabbed hold of the duvet, threw himself across the bed and flung the duvet over the pelican. It struggled and heaved with such strength that Gerald had to lie right across it to hold it down.

The bedroom door burst open. 'It's nine o'clock!' cried Gerald's mother. 'And it's Saturday. There's so much to do today. Remember Romoana Sneedie, Gerald?'

'How could one ever forget her?' muttered the pelican.

Gerald's mother said, 'Pardon, dear?'

'Nothing really, Mum,' said Gerald, pressing hard where he thought the pelican's beak might be.

'Oh. Well, I just wanted to remind you that the fight is on again today.' She marched across the room and drew back the curtains. She turned back again and said, 'Gerald? Get up off that bed, Gerald!'

'Right, Mum,' said Gerald. He stayed exactly where he was.

'Gerald, don't be so disobedient. Get up this minute!'

Gerald wondered what he could do. He would just have to get up and let the pelican flap out from under the duvet, and then . . .

'What a dreadful fishy smell!' cried his mother, sniffing. 'It's coming from over here.' She advanced towards the bed and bent over, still sniffing. When she stood up again she was holding her nose with one hand and a pair of Gerald's football socks with

the other. 'Really, Gerald,' she said. 'These socks must have been stinking away here for days.'

Still holding her nose and the socks, Gerald's mother went out of the room.

Gerald lay on his bed and listened to her muttering as she went downstairs. Then he realized that the pelican had not moved for at least three minutes. He must have squashed it flat, or smothered it with the duvet. He stared at the lump which lay on his bed. Could you give a pelican the kiss of life?

All of a sudden, out shot the pelican's head with its bright, beady eye. 'Boo!' it said. It flopped down on to the floor and waddled towards the door, after Gerald's mother.

'Stop, pelican!' cried Gerald.

And it did.

'I apologize for the incident with the goldfish,' it said. 'My instinct almost got the better of me.' It stretched out its neck and hummed to itself as it read the titles of Gerald's bookshelves. '*Wings Over the Waves*. That sounds an excellent book, Gerald.'

'It's about seaplanes, not birds,' said Gerald. 'Now then, I am going downstairs to have my breakfast. I'm going to shut you in here, pelican. Don't you dare do anything bad.'

'I wouldn't dream of it, Gerald,' said the pelican. It turned its head, so that its marble eye gleamed.

CHAPTER TWO

Gerald's mother had felt too nervous to eat breakfast that morning. His father had gone into work, even though it was Saturday. Gerald was sure he had gone so that he wouldn't get dragged off to the campaign. Gerald's father was easily embarrassed, especially by Gerald's mother. And he had once whispered to Gerald that he'd rather face six pit-bull terriers wearing rattlesnakes as collars than Romoana S. Gerald thought that his dad was being particularly wimpish. Romoana Sneedie was only a woman. Not that Gerald had ever met her . . .

So Gerald ate his breakfast alone.

At least, he thought he was alone.

Halfway through his fourth slice of toast and black-cherry jam, he heard a flip-flop, slithering sound. He looked up to see the pelican flip-flop slithering down the stairs. It must have opened the door by pulling the handle with the hook on its beak.

The pelican waddled over to a cupboard, opened it and swept something off a shelf with its wing. 'Kindly open them, Gerald,' it said. 'I do like them in tomato sauce. It's a pity they're not already in tomato sauce in the sea, really.'

Gerald opened the tin of sardines.

The pelican said, 'Spoon them in, please,' and opened its beak. Gerald spooned in the sardines. They slid down into the dark, gaping pouch.

17

The pelican swallowed with a great GLURP. Then it put its head on one side.

'That's my mother vacuuming,' said Gerald. 'She's nervous. She doesn't know what to do next. Sometimes before a protest I find her polishing the light bulbs or my dad's head.'

'Your mother is a heroine,' said the pelican. 'I hope to work with her this time. Direct action, Gerald, that's the name of the game. Some might call it guerrilla warfare. They know a thing or two.'

'Who?'

'The gorillas. We're all in it together. We're all endangered.'

'What can you do, pelican? You can't vote or go on marches,' said Gerald.

'Do not underestimate me, Gerald,' warned the pelican. 'I have been detailed by my committee to aid your mother in the struggle on behalf of my freshwater brothers. The future of many mallards, coots and moorhens depends on me. They remember the Riverside Massacre and tremble at the very name of Sneedie. I would die for them, Gerald.'

The pelican puffed itself up and preened its feathers so that its beak made a clapping noise like hedge-clippers. Gerald realized that it came right up to his shoulder. It was not a bird to ignore.

'It's all a yawn, this protest stuff,' muttered Gerald. 'It's all over the telly and the papers. People like Mum get their knickers in a twist, but nothing awful really happens. Not in this town. Mum spent weeks standing around trying to save a bit of boring old grass for some butterfly or insect that you never see anyway.'

'You could be talking about my food chain, Gerald,' warned the pelican.

'Sardines seem more your cup of tea,' said Gerald, putting the can in the bin for tins by the back door. (There was also a bottle bin, a compost bin, a paper pile and a bucket for bits which didn't fit into any obvious category.) Then he cleared the table and squeezed plenty of washing-up liquid into the sink. Soon it was full of frothy white bubbles.

The pelican squawked, 'Lift me up, Gerald.'

Gerald did as he was told. The pelican was warm and soft and very heavy.

'Put me on the draining board,' it commanded. And there it sat, looking down into the sink with its large, ringed eyes. 'Where are they?' it squawked.

'Where are what?' asked Gerald.

'The fish, of course. I see water, I see bubbles, but I don't see fish,' it snapped.

Gerald sighed. 'Fish don't live in washing-up water,' he said.

'I challenge your assumption,' said the pelican, and it flopped down into the sink with such a splash that the bubbles surged out over the top and began to spread out in a glistening white mass across the kitchen floor.

The pelican stamped about in the sink, displacing more bubbles and stabbing its beak in and out as if it were an oar. There was a dreadful breaking sound.

Gerald suddenly realized that the vacuuming had stopped. He grabbed the saturated bird and heaved it right out of the sink. Water poured from its feathers and it struggled and hissed and scratched so much with its great rough feet that he dropped it just as the kitchen door opened. Gerald stuffed the soggy, scrabbling mass inside his dressing-gown as his mother said, 'What was all that noise? And there's that fishy smell again, like the chip shop on a Friday night.'

Gerald backed towards the stairs.

'Where did all this water come from?' cried his mother. 'Did you make all this mess, Gerald?'

'No,' he answered truthfully. He set off upstairs, clutching a cold, wet pelican to his chest.

'You were right after all,' muttered

a small voice close to Gerald's heart. 'Fish don't live in washing-up water.'

'What did you say?' shouted Gerald's mum. 'Am I supposed to clear all this mess up? And . . . oh no! Gerald, you have broken everything in this sink. Even the dear little Pooh and Piglet mug that Auntie Hermione gave you is broken.'

'Oh dear,' smiled Gerald. 'The water must have been too hot. Now, pelican,' he whispered, 'just behave yourself!'

'Of course, Gerald,' it said. 'But whether I behave myself well or whether I behave myself badly remains to be seen.'

CHAPTER THREE

Gerald untied the cord of his dressing-gown and the pelican tumbled on to the carpet in a heap of wet feathers. It shook itself and drops of water flew around the room. 'Where does your mother's protest begin today?' it asked.

'Dunno. She said it's somewhere near the High Street, I think.'

The pelican brightened. 'Is there a – what do you call it? – a fishmonger in this lofty street, Gerald? I am an easy bird to please. I like cod and coley when times are hard, but haddock, halibut, herring and hake please my palate more. I also enjoy red mullet, grey mullet, skate with black butter, and plaice. I have a weakness for Dover sole, and have been known to enjoy prawns and crab. If properly served, lobster is also acceptable.'

'Oh, is it?' said Gerald. 'Well, you won't get the chance to turn your beak up or down at anything, because there's no fishmonger where we're going. You can have a pilchard when we get back, if you're lucky.'

The pelican took umbrage. It ruffled its feathers and snapped, 'The secret briefing in the diplomatic pouch said my mission was the saving of a pool. Not a High Street without a fishmonger.'

'Don't blame me,' Gerald snapped back. 'I don't know where the silly woman's going. I just have to tag along behind.'

He dressed quickly and went downstairs, with the pelican slithering after him.

'I don't care for stairs,' it complained.

'I'm not carrying you down as well as up,' said Gerald.

'I've got legs. I can use them,' it snapped.

'You've got wings, too,' said Gerald.

'It is extremely difficult, well nigh impossible, for me to take off in such restricted space,' announced the pelican.

'Our house isn't that small,' said Gerald.

'I've seen bigger houses when prison-visiting in your zoos,' it said.

'I do wish you'd stop talking to yourself and put your anorak on, Gerald,' called his mum. She grabbed her fold-up Go-Anywhere Protest Placard and off they went, Gerald having to run and the pelican struggling along behind, squawking, 'Don't get in such a flap, woman.' It finally caught them up at the crossing with the little green man.

'Look! There's a pelican crossing,' sniggered Gerald.

They had to run for the bus. The

pelican flopped on to the platform just in time and heaved itself upstairs. Its beak was wide open and it was panting. Gerald followed, thinking it was a good job the pelican had no heavy shopping to carry.

'Why don't you want to sit downstairs?' he asked.

'I prefer to be high in the sky, low in the sea, or asleep,' it said. 'I would feel insecure downstairs.'

'I'm glad you're coming on the protest with us,' said Gerald, and the pelican lifted and settled the tuft on top of its head with pleasure. 'Today is going to be another wasted Saturday,' Gerald went on. 'Mum thinks that coming with her makes me a better boy, socially conscious and environmentally aware and all that rubbish.'

'Your mother is a champion of feather and scale,' proclaimed the pelican. 'She is our true ally.'

'Ally? Dad says she's mad,' said Gerald. 'He says Romoana Sneedie is one of the mighty, rich and powerful. He says people like Mum can never defeat her.'

'Perhaps people on their own cannot,' said the pelican. 'But people plus pelican may.'

'Gerald? GERALD! Here we are!' cried his mum from downstairs. 'You keep talking to yourself,' she said as she struggled to get her placard out from the cubby-hole under the stairs, poking the conductor up the nose with the handle. 'I'm so sorry . . . But Gerald, there is another noise – I don't know if you realize you're making it or if I should contact a child psychiatrist . . . it's a sort of muttering and hissing sound, like radio interference.'

'Oh that,' said Gerald. 'I'm just practising spellings and seventeen-times tables for a test on Monday.'

His mother did not look convinced.

The pelican flip-flop slithered down from the platform after them and landed in an ungainly heap in the gutter.

'This is where the action is,' cried Mum.

'Action? You could have fooled me,' grumbled Gerald. There they all were, he thought, the same old do-gooders in their brown anoraks. The odd toddler who wasn't old enough yet to have words to complain was strapped tightly into the odd pushchair. There were no other *boys*, of course. Other *boys* were doing exciting Saturday things like lying in bed, spending money or drowning stupid girls in the local swimming pool. Other boys with real mothers didn't have to stand and protest.

Mind you, Gerald realized, they'd chosen a better location this Saturday. It was the local playground. Sometimes he and his mother came here after they'd been to the supermarket.

'I wonder why we're here,' he said to the pelican. 'The toddler part, with the diddy roundabout and see-saw and those spotty pigs and horses they bounce on, is dead babyish. But that slide is terrific, the swings are fine, and the rope rigging is great. Fancy a slide?'

The pelican's marble eye gleamed and it shuffled over to the slide. It struggled up the steps with Gerald pushing from behind. Then it whizzed down the slide, wings wide, its beak open to let out a hiss of excitement like air escaping from a tyre. Gerald slid right behind and they landed in a heap, giggling.

Suddenly the pelican stopped rolling around. Its feathers stood on end. 'She is coming,' it said.

Everyone was crowding round the playground gate. Gerald's mum was in front. She raised her placard. It said:

WE REFUSE TO LOSE OUR
SWINGS AND ROUNDABOUTS.
HANDS OFF OUR
PLAYGROUND

'Eh?' said Gerald. 'How can you lose a playground?' He ran up to his mum, who was talking to a policeman.

'Gerald, this is the new bobby on the beat,' she said.

'Hello, son. I'm PC Nick M. Smartish,' cried the constable, beaming all round. 'I'm fresh in these parts. I'm all for the people, of course, but I'm here to clean up this town.'

'It's only a one-horse town, Sheriff,' said Gerald. 'Nothing much happens.'

'Ah, law and order is the name of the game, son,' cried PC Smartish. 'And the town's First Lady is about to arrive.'

'Some lady!' snapped Gerald's mum.

'She is nigh,' hissed the pelican, peering through the constable's legs.

A large black limousine swished up out of nowhere and purred to a halt. An electric window slid down. Gerald could see only darkness. A chauffeur hurried to open the door.

Out slid an arm, bearing a big red snakeskin handbag. Out slid a pair of great red snakeskin shoes with stiletto heels that would rip your floors to shreds.

In the horrible red shoes were the huge feet belonging on the ends of the legs belonging to Romoana Sneedie.

The boos of the crowd died away as she stood before them, smiling.

CHAPTER FOUR

Romoana Sneedie was taller than Gerald's mum, much taller. She was surrounded by a forcefield of perfume that reminded Gerald of flyspray. Her eyes were like blue glass. Her hair was yellow and tacky with spray, as if she had bought it at the candyfloss stall. On top of the yellow candyfloss was perched a little blue velvet hat, crescent-shaped like a tiara. She wore a shiny blouse with a big chocolate-box bow tied under her chin, and a suit of blue waffle-finish fabric with huge shoulders and a fur collar.

'That fur should have stayed on the rat, madam,' hissed the pelican.

'How charming of you all to meet me!' breathed Romoana.

Her voice was the worst thing about her. It was a pretend voice, soft and smothering as a foam pillow. Gerald knew that at any moment it could shriek louder than a dentist's drill at full dig.

'Good morning, Councillor Sneedie,' said Gerald's mum. 'A good friend of mine at the Council offices heard about your takeover of the playground and tipped us off. It's outrageous! I don't understand how you got on the Council, anyway. Everyone I ask says they certainly didn't vote for you. Now you're depriving us of our playground.'

'You must understand, my dear, that we need this playground far more than you do,' breathed Romoana Sneedie, her head on one side as if she were talking to a two year old.

'Rubbish, Councillor. All the families in this town need that playground for leisure and exercise. Many of them live in flats without gardens and they can't afford slides and swings, anyway.'

'That's right,' piped up a voice which Gerald heard with surprise. 'We poor deprived little kiddies want to whizz round on the roundabout and bounce on the spotty little horses.'

The voice was Gerald's. He felt tears pricking his eyelids. (Actually, Gerald had a big garden with a climbing frame and swing, but he hoped he looked deprived.)

Romoana Sneedie leered down at him. Her eyes glinted like glacier mints.

'Your parent is obviously not setting you a good example, sonny,' she sneered. 'Little boys shouldn't meddle in politics. Not against *me*, anyway. Why aren't you at home in front of a video?'

'Because Mum wouldn't let me,' was on Gerald's lips, but then he felt a great surge of anger. How dare this person with her feet shod in snakeskin say his mum wasn't a fit parent? How dare she call him 'sonny'? He felt angry and humiliated.

The next thing Gerald felt was a pat on the head. It wasn't a gentle pat. It hurt.

The pat came from a little man with a round red face and half-moon spectacles. He made Gerald think of a lollipop. The lollipop was wearing a hairy tweed suit that looked as if it would scratch if you brushed against it.

'Boys like you should be off the streets or locked away in an institution,' said the lollipop. 'Short-sharp-shock treatment and all that.'

'I've already had the short sharp shock,' grumbled Gerald, rubbing his sore head.

'Allow me to introduce my husband Norris,' gushed Romoana. 'He is Chairman of Sneedie Enterprises and a director on the boards of countless other firms.'

'On the board? More like under the

table,' said Gerald's mum. 'He *stinks* of whisky.'

Romoana ignored this and cried, 'We do thank you all for coming, and I'm sure you're all pleased that the Council have sold the playground. It's nice to see your jolly little placards, although I don't care for the one that says "SNUB THE SNEEDIES".'

'We're here to protest,' cried a big man with twins in a double buggy.

'The Council have sold the only place we can safely take our toddlers. They haven't all got slides and swings in their gardens. In fact, some of them haven't even got gardens.'

'Well, that's their fault,' replied Romoana. She bent down and leered at the twins. 'You may play for a few hours yet. Auntie Romoana says so. Play your hardest, my cherubs.'

The twins in the double buggy stared back at Romoana Sneedie without blinking. Then they both stuck out their bright pink tongues.

'Make a note, Norris, that some kind of Nursery National Service is needed for subversive toddlers,' snapped Romoana. 'Now, I must be gone. I have a top-level meeting with Mr I.M.A. Greedyfeller. He is a colleague from Texas. A magnate. And I don't mean the horseshoe kind. Goodbye. I'm sure we'll all meet again soon.'

'We certainly will!' roared Gerald's mum and her friends.

Romoana Sneedie folded herself into the car and Norris scrambled in after her. The windows whizzed, the engine purred, and Gerald caught sight of something like the inside of a feather pillow heaving itself up into the boot.

'I can't believe anyone would get the Council to sell off a little kids' playground,' said Gerald.

'The Sneedies would,' said his mother sadly. 'There's obviously something in it for them.'

'There's nothing you can do if she's got it all signed, sealed and delivered,' said PC Smartish. 'It's a shame, really, though I shouldn't say so.'

'What's next, then?' asked Gerald, itching to follow the big black car.

'Next?' whispered his mother, shaking her head in bewilderment. Then she rallied and said, 'Fish and chips all round. That's what's next.'

CHAPTER FIVE

'I'll get them,' cried Gerald. 'Just tell me what to buy and give me the money. I'll be delivery boy today.'

'Oh, thank you, love,' said his mother. She handed him a note. 'Fancy you volunteering. Fancy you being enthusiastic about anything. Well, get twelve lots of chips, and six fish. Whatever looks nice and fresh. And salt and vinegar and . . .'

Gerald was off down the High Street as fast as his feet could carry him. 'It's a good job it's Saturday and there's lots of traffic to slow down the Sneediemobile,' he said. 'Trouble is, all these Saturday shoppers slow me down, too. Sorry, sorry, sorry,' he called as people tutted and moaned as he pushed past them.

This is real private-detective work, he thought. I could hail a taxi and say, 'Follow that pelican'.

He could see the black limousine ahead at the traffic lights. He puffed up alongside just as the lights changed. It purred away. Gerald heard a voice from somewhere cackle, 'What a pity you have only got those primitive kind of feet, Gerald. Wings are a far superior method of transport.'

The car overtook a bus loading passengers at a bus stop, and Gerald lost sight of it. He began to panic. He knew that the number plate said SNEE D1, but what good was that when he was on foot and the limousine could do a ton? What would happen if it went on the motorway?

Ah! There it was, turning left down a side street. Gerald put on an extra spurt and turned the corner after it.

In the little street he bent double, gasping for breath. He wasn't a fan of physical fitness and he had a horrible stitch pain in his side. When he straightened up he saw the Sneediemobile parked outside the Hotel Splendide (two stars). He tiptoed up to the car and peered inside.

Norris Sneedie was asleep on the back seat with his mouth wide open.

There was no Romoana and no pelican. Further up the street, the chauffeur was disappearing into a newsagent's shop.

'Action!' cried Gerald and ricocheted through the swing doors of Hotel Splendide, only to find that it was not. It was dingy, with toffee-coloured varnish all over the walls, and dirty yellow carpet on the floor. There was a smell of stale tobacco smoke with a faint suggestion of something else. Gerald sniffed. Yes . . . Romoana Sneedie's fly-killing perfume.

'Easy-peasy catchee Sneedie,' whispered Gerald. 'But where is that pelican?'

He hurried into the dining-room. Luncheon was finished. Gerald saw on the menu that luncheon had been mutton-and-cabbage pizza, followed by Spotted Dick Splendide and custard.

'Nothing to your liking here, pelican,' he muttered.

He glanced into the lounge. There was only a woman asleep in a swollen armchair with a bowl of cold Spotted Dick on the table beside her.

Gerald even checked in the gents. No pelican. As he came out, he heard someone shouting, 'Lance? LANCE!' and darted to hide behind a big pot of plastic ferns that looked fierce enough to eat you.

'Yeah, yeah, just got me feet up,' groaned a voice from behind the desk.

Gerald saw the soles of the shoes up on the desk and heard the voice moan, 'I'm just watching *Grot Grove Omnibus*. I want to know if Mrs Doddle runs off with the man from the A.A.'

'Mrs Sneedie and the Texan want room service, and I'm just going off duty,' went on the first voice. 'Take it up, Lance. She's in the Suite Splendide on the first floor. Bye!'

There was no answer.

Gerald's heart raced. There by the desk was a hostess trolley with an ice bucket and a domed silver tureen, all ready for Romoana. And there behind the desk (rumour had it) was Lance, deep in *Grot Grove Omnibus* which – Gerald glanced at his watch – would be on for another half an hour or so.

And there on top of the desk sat Lance's cap. It was black, with bits of gold braid dangling off, and the name of the hotel with the 'D's' missing.

Dare I? thought Gerald.

He dare.

He took off his anorak and stuffed it

down inside the big plastic fern. Then he tiptoed over to the desk and put on the cap. It fell right down over his eyes.

Just as well. I need some disguise – she might remember me from this morning, he thought.

He pushed the cap up far enough to see where he was going and set off with the trolley. Luckily, it didn't squeak. He pushed it into the lift and whizzed up to the first floor and then down the dim corridor to the door of Suite Splendide.

He passed no pelican.

Gerald was beginning to fear for its safety. Perhaps Romoana Sneedie had kidnapped – or should that be chicknapped – the pelican. Gerald imagined it crouched forlornly behind bars in Wormwood Scrubs, a bare fishbone at its feet.

He knocked timidly on the door, then again, more loudly.

'Come on in, bell-hop!' roared a voice, and Gerald trundled in, past a door open into a bathroom, and into the main room.

Either side of a table with gold squirly legs sat Romoana Sneedie and a tall man in a white stetson. They stared at him. Gerald noticed that Romoana had sloshed on a lot of lipstick and looked as if she'd just eaten a blood-flavoured ice lolly.

The big man had clothes kinda like a cowboy's, but they were clean and creased in the right places. Gerald decided he hadn't been within five miles of a cow in them – certainly not within five miles of a cowpat. His boots were of white polished leather with high heels and tassels on the back. Wow!

'Room service,' grunted Gerald, hoping he sounded like the invisible Lance.

Neither of them even said 'thank you'. The man took the bottle of champagne from the ice bucket and poured two very full glasses. He handed one of them to Romoana.

They had forgotten him, Gerald

realized, and he backed away towards the door. But instead of going out into the corridor, he side-stepped into the bathroom to spy on them.

'Success has made me very hungry,' announced Romoana. She stood up and lifted the lid on the big tureen.

Gerald's knees turned to jelly.

Underneath, surrounded by roast potatoes, peas, carrots and a thick moat of gravy, was a large, golden, thoroughly roasted bird.

CHAPTER SIX

'How could they!' sobbed Gerald, through the lump in his throat. He watched Romoana pick up a knife and begin to saw away at the big bird's legs, which were sticking up in the air. 'And how did they get him cooked so quickly? He wouldn't fit in a microwave.'

He stepped backwards to get away from the hideous sight and tripped over a heap of something on the floor. An indignant squawking echoed around the bathroom.

'Do be careful, Gerald!' snapped the pelican. 'It is bad enough to witness those murderers feasting upon that unfortunate turkey, without another of their kind standing on my webs.'

'Of course, Americans are into turkey!' cried Gerald with relief.

'One learns something new every day,' said the pelican. 'Well, Gerald, *I* am into justice for the bird world, including my farmyard brothers.'

'I'm sorry,' said Gerald, feeling humble. 'But try not to squawk too loudly or they'll hear us, even though they're munching on that, er. . . How did you get here, pelican?'

'With extreme difficulty, Gerald. I followed her in, but stairs are not my forte and I cannot manage lift buttons, because I have no fingers. So I took a ride in the laundry basket. No-one noticed me. I toppled out when my extra-acute senses detected Sneedie's smell and song. And terrible they are too.'

Gerald said nothing. He was finding the pelican's own personal aroma a bit much in that tiny bathroom. It was like being in a heap of old herring on a hot afternoon.

'Now then, Gerald, we must listen, learn and then consider our strategy,' advised the pelican. 'Some favour the teachings of Gandhi Guillemot, but one can end up as a nasty mess of feathers if one lies down in peaceful protest. Others follow the ways of the Vigilante Vulture. Especially as your species takes more and more for itself. If I could choose, I would like to be considered as a twentieth-century Robin Pouch, taking from the Sneedie and giving to the needy.'

'Perhaps you will be,' said Gerald. 'I must say, I'm enjoying being a private detective.'

'I'm an old wing at it,' said the pelican.

'Let's listen, old wing,' said Gerald, and they peered round the door.

The man in the stetson was grasping a turkey drumstick and tearing off pieces of flesh with his teeth. Romoana toyed with a pea. She said, 'Mr Greedyfeller . . . Irvin. I can't tell you how delightful this is. And how delightful it will be when we've built the luxury hotel and leisure complex on the ruins of this town. It will be beyond our wildest dreams – and beyond most people's pockets, except the very, very rich. And they are the ones who always suffer!'

'Of course, my dear Romoana,' drawled Irvin Greedyfeller, and he bent down so the strings of his purple bootlace tie dangled in the gravy. 'We'll have the freedom to eat lobster, quail and sweet little baby chickens in my penthouse suite. I'll have a roulette wheel in the jacuzzi and a hotline to my private safari park. Then I can phone to check there are enough leopards for me to shoot at the weekend. And I'm going to call it Hotel Romoana.'

'How charming,' she simpered. 'I think Norris might be a little jealous. But he hasn't made quite so much money lately, so that's his own fault. I have the paper for you to sign, Irvin.' She took a roll of paper, tied with a ribbon, from the pocket of her red snakeskin bag. 'The Council soon agreed to sell the land,' she said. 'They haven't any money at the moment and they're worried they may have to close a few old people's homes and some schools. Nothing important. I said you were willing to buy the playground and the park with the duckpond.'

'The duckpond!' hissed Gerald. 'So that's why you're here!'

The pelican closed its eyes to show agreement.

'Do you know, the Council think we're going to keep the playground and pond going, Irvin? They don't know we're going to send in the personal roadroller Norris bought me for Christmas. It's a huge vintage with a roller that will flatten everything in sight. It will grind all those little horses and slides and roundabouts into the ground.' She laughed, and her eyes rolled like blue gobstoppers.

'I adore cunning women,' said Irvin Greedyfeller. 'How did you manage to get all the councillors' signatures?'

'Well, I showed them the cash you had given me – nothing like the true worth of the land, of course. Then I gave them each a slice of my home-made prune-and-molasses gâteau. They just had to make their minds up and go! They really weren't sure what they were signing, the fools. Now, if you sign here, where it says "sold to" . . .'

'Sure thing, ma'am. Let's see . . .' He took out a gold pen. 'I.M.A. Greedyfeller. There we are, Romoana.'

'I'm so looking forward to my share of the profits you promised me,' she gushed. 'We'll make lots of money together. When are you flying back to Texas?'

'After I've seen this thing through with you this afternoon,' said I.M.A. Greedyfeller. 'And after we've drunk all the champagne and picked all the meat off this tough old bird.'

Romoana rolled up the document, tied the red ribbon around it and put it in the side pocket of her handbag. She frowned as she watched Irvin filling her glass to the brim. She hooked her handbag over her arm, picked up the glass and said, '*Do* excuse me a moment, Irvin,' and wobbled off on her high heels.

Two heads ducked back into the bathroom.

'She's coming in here, pelican!' hissed Gerald. 'Help!'

CHAPTER SEVEN

The pelican shut its eyes tight and tucked its beak and feet in under the bundle of its body.

Gerald leaped into the shower and pulled the curtain across just as Romoana Sneedie swept into the bathroom.

Gerald's heart sank. He really didn't want to see her on the loo. What a nightmare. But she headed instead for the washbasin. She put down her handbag and her glass. Then she leered at herself in the mirror, so that Gerald hoped it would crack.

She said, 'I don't think we'll

drink any more champagne, do you, Romoana? I think we'll keep a clear head. After all, I have the photographer coming to the pond, and I may get riff-raff asking awkward questions about the sale.'

Gerald heard a strange hissing sound. There it was again! He interpreted the hissing as 'Get that paper, Fingers!'

'What strange sounds these old water pipes and ancient plumbing make,' commented Romoana, as Gerald's arm snaked round from behind the shower curtain, tweaked the paper out of the pocket of the red bag and snaked back round to his own pocket.

'In fact,' announced Romoana, lips pursed as she slathered on more blood-coloured lipstick, 'this hotel is a disgrace.'

She picked up her bag and stepped towards the door, catching her heel in the heap of pelican as she went.

This is it, thought Gerald, imagining pelican steaks in the Sneedie deep-freeze.

'Eugh! How disgusting!' shrieked Romoana. 'Just look at that filthy old bath towel. It should be burned for reasons of hygiene alone. Standards here are the lowest of the low.'

Romoana left.

The pelican stayed flattened against the floor.

At last its head crept out. It swallowed and spoke in a small voice. 'A filthy old bath towel? Not a very suave image, Gerald, is it?' It tried to laugh and failed. Gerald didn't know what to say. After all, you couldn't pretend that the pelican had the shimmering beauty of the peacock or the snowy elegance of the swan.

Gerald took a deep breath and said, 'Pelican, you are unique. It's the inner bird that counts, after all.'

The pelican raised the crest on the top of its head. 'Thank you, Gerald,' it said graciously. It stood up, fluffed out its feathers and preened its chest. Then it glared at the glass of champagne. 'I've always wondered what this is like,' it squawked, and drank the lot before Gerald could stop it. 'Needs more salt,' it complained.

'I don't think you should have done that. You've no head for drink,' cried Gerald.

'When in Rome,' it retorted.

Gerald pushed it towards the door, whispering, 'Let's get out of here.' It swayed as he pushed it into the corridor and then it burped, waving a wing in front of its beak. Gerald had to roll it into the lift where it burst into 'Shons of the Shea' and then fell on its back, cackling.

'More shampagne, Mrs Shneedie!' it squawked.

Gerald grabbed hold of the pelican's big rough feet and dragged it through the hall, putting back Lance's cap on the desk as they passed. The title music of *Grot Grove Omnibus* was playing.

'Just in time!' gasped Gerald as he dragged the bird out into the sunlight. 'You're sozzled!' he snapped. 'And we've still got to get rid of the Sneedie-Greedyfeller agreement. You've dropped me in it, pelican.'

'Gerald, dear boy, I'm shobering up rapido!' it squawked, and righted itself so that it swayed before him on the pavement. 'There's life in the old bath towel yet!' It began to dance.

'We need a dustbin,' said Gerald firmly.

'No, Gerald. We need some ink.

Onwards to the High Street!' it commanded and rollicked away ahead of Gerald, teetering on the kerb and falling in the gutter.

Gerald hurried along behind. 'All we need is you to be arrested for being drunk and disorderly!' he snapped.

The pelican pretended not to hear. It stopped in the doorway of the office supplies shop, swayed and fell in through the door which swung open, *dinged* loudly and deposited the pelican on the carpet inside.

'May I help you?' asked a salesman, approaching Gerald who was standing in the doorway with his mouth hanging open.

'Err-I-ummm...' stuttered Gerald, and a voice from the floor hissed, 'Corrector fluid.'

'What?' frowned Gerald.

'I said CORRECTOR FLUID!' snapped the pelican, and Gerald felt the stab of its beak in the back of his knee. He stamped hard where he hoped its web might be, but missed.

'I'd like some corrector fluid, please,' he said, rubbing his stinging leg.

'Certainly,' said the salesman, taking a little bottle of white liquid from the shelf behind him. Gerald paid with some of his precious pocket money.

'Thank you,' said the salesman. 'Oh – please excuse me. There's the phone.'

'I've got a headache,' grumbled the pelican.

'Serves you right,' said Gerald. 'Now then, what do I do?'

'First, take out the document.'

'Ye-es!'

'Then take the corrector fluid in your right hand and paint out Irvin Greedyfeller's signature. Also, paint out the amount he paid the Council for the playground and the pond. But pray be careful, Gerald. Not too much white gunge. We must avoid detection.'

'I hope we're doing the right thing,' said Gerald anxiously.

'That is an interesting philosophical and moral matter,' said the pelican. 'But my pouch reaction is that we are certainly doing the right thing for the good of the many. Sneedie and Greedyfeller are acting immorally.'

'And they don't like birds.'

'And they don't like birds. Now, take one of my very best feathers, Gerald. Here!' It hoiked out a feather from its wing and beaked it to Gerald.

'What's this for?'

'It's a quill, to write with. I have no fingers, Gerald, and my writing is illegible. Of course, we have other ways of communication, unknown to human beings. Our thoughts merge on occasion.'

'Well,' said Gerald, 'I usually use a pen . . . I don't suppose anyone has used a quill for years.'

'It's the real way, Gerald,' advised the pelican. 'I trust you have a penknife? Sharpen my feather, then just dip it carefully into that bottle of blue ink. Now listen, Gerald, as I dictate.'

And Gerald listened and wrote in his best handwriting everything that the pelican dictated.

'Now we need a personal web-print for verification,' it announced, and wobbled on one leg while holding the other scaly foot up near Gerald's face. 'Ink this, please,' it said.

'No fear,' said Gerald. 'Look, we'll use that stamp pad. Much less mess.'

He grabbed the web and pressed it against the stamp pad. Then he stamped the inky web down on to a space in the document and held it there to get a good clear print. The pelican wobbled and fell over backwards.

'What a performance,' sighed Gerald. 'Can we go now?'

'Let us be cautious,' said the pelican, scrambling up. It wobbled across the shop, flopped up on to an office chair and helped itself to something from the table. It turned round and beckoned Gerald. He saw that it wore a pair of horn-rimmed spectacles.

'Those aren't yours. Put them back!' cried Gerald. His mother sometimes came into this shop to buy paper, and he didn't want to get into trouble.

'I think these spectacles are obligatory for anyone who wants to use this machine,' it announced, waving a wing at the photocopier. It pushed off from the table and spun round on the steel chair, squawking with excitement.

Gerald felt dizzy watching it. I'm

dizzy through hunger, he thought, as hundreds of pelicans whizzed past him.

It swivelled to a halt and shrieked, 'Gerald, am I or am I not a twentieth-century, hi-tech bird?'

Gerald sighed. 'Yes, pelican. You're hi-tech all right,' he muttered. Anything for a quiet life.

'Now then, let us take a copy of the document just to be on the safe side,' it said briskly. 'After all, you never know when dishonest folk are around. And we can keep a copy after the real one is returned.'

'Returned?' squeaked Gerald. 'Who by?'

'You, of course. Romoana Sneedie will become suspicious if it's not returned, and she'll draw up another. Now then, Gerald, pay for the copy.'

'Humph!' sulked Gerald. He took a copy and left the twenty pence. Then he carefully rolled up the original and turned to go. 'Be careful!' he cried to the bird, who was teetering above the photocopier. 'Don't fall in or you'll get trapped.'

Its eyes were gleaming with excitement as if it were glaring down into the sea from the edge of a cliff.

'This technology is such fun, Gerald,' it hissed. 'Fear not. I'm only photocopying that feather. You know, the one I pulled out to use as a quill.'

'Er – how many times?' asked Gerald.

'Hmmmm . . . Let me see . . . What did I request? Two thousand,' it said. 'Is that many?'

'Let's go!' said Gerald, and he ran for the door.

CHAPTER EIGHT

'I don't see how I can get it back into her handbag,' whispered Gerald as he crouched behind the big plant pot. 'I can't be Lance again. He's wearing his cap himself. Look, you can just see it the other side. He's talking to the chambermaid.'

'It were there, waiting,' floated Lance's voice over the desk counter. 'The trolley were all piled up with roast turkey and champers. "Take it to the Sneedie woman and him in the stetson in the Suite Splendide," says the boss. "Yes," I says, "at the end of *Grot Grove Omnibus*." But at the end of *Grot Grove* it were gone. Then they rings down from S.S. to say "Fetch it back, bell-hop." I think this hotel is haunted, that's what I think. The Sneedie woman says to me, "You've grown in the last few minutes." Cheek. I was forty-five last birthday.'

'Now then, Gerald, human beings are supposed to be inventive,' said the pelican. 'How will you get Romoana's document back to her?'

'Why me?' hissed Gerald.

'Because I can't get up there on my own,' snapped the pelican.

'Right, I'll take you there, tucked under my arm,' said Gerald. 'I know! I'll pretend to be from Interflora. You can hide behind my legs and stuff the document back in her bag. There's only one snag.'

'And what, pray, is that?'

'There's no flora for us to inter.'

'Simple, my dear boy,' it said loftily, and wrenched off the plastic fern in the nearby pot with its beak. Then it yanked out some of the surrounding faded roses. 'Poof! Dust!' it complained. 'I like to woo my females with an anchovy or a pouchful of choice eel. Your habits are quaint. Now, Gerald, gather them into a bouquet and head for the lift.'

'Yes, your lordship,' said Gerald. He stuffed the dusty flowers under one arm and tried to carry the pelican under the other. It was far too bulky and fell just before they reached the lift. It waddled swiftly inside, hissing, 'I shall endeavour to remain inconspicuous as always.'

'Difficult,' said Gerald. He tucked the document in the pelican's beak.

This time, Gerald banged loudly on the door of the Suite Splendide. At once Irvin Greedyfeller called, 'Come on in.'

Gerald held the dirty plastic bouquet high before his face. Romoana and the American were still sitting at the table. This time, a box of luscious chocolates lay open before them. Gerald's mouth watered. Perhaps they'll offer me one, he thought.

'Interflora,' he muttered. Out of the corner of his eye he saw the horrible red snakeskin bag on the floor by the table leg and felt the feathers of the pelican as it brushed past him.

'Interflora? How charming,' gushed Romoana, and Gerald thrust the bouquet towards her. 'But how extraordinary. They are unusual to say the least. And they seem to be covered in some kind of grey pollen. They must be from somewhere exotic . . . Who sent them, boy?'

'Um. . .er. . .me?' mumbled Gerald.

'Don't be silly! And what grammar! I mean, where is the card?'

The card! They had forgotten the card. Gerald remembered now that when his dad sent his mum flowers for her birthday, they always had a card, saying things like, 'To my action lady, from your adoring diddikins, Norm.'

'I think they're from an unknown admirer,' said Gerald. 'He wants to remain secret. Anonymous.'

Romoana Sneedie's eyes grew cold as glass. 'Haven't I seen you somewhere before?' she said. 'Don't I remember you?'

Gerald didn't wait to find out. He cried, 'Much obliged, Madam!' and ran for it, the pelican gasping at his heels, out into the corridor, down in the lift, through the entrance hall, back to the plantless pot to snatch up his anorak, and out into the street. They collapsed in a heap on the pavement.

When it could speak, the pelican said, 'Mission accomplished, comrade. Or rather, friend.'

'Great,' said Gerald. He stood up. Norris Sneedie was still asleep in the back of the limousine, and the chauffeur sprawled in front, listening to the racing on the car radio.

'It seems ages since I went out for fish and chips,' Gerald said. 'Hear that, friend? We are now going somewhere you will like very much indeed. It will be a just reward for your little act of espionage. We are going to the fish-and-chip shop!'

The pelican performed one of its odd little dance routines, slapping its feet on the pavement and making a noise as if a kettle was boiling deep inside its pouch. Once inside Freda's Fry-Up its eyes glittered as it watched Freda in her tiny white trilby, held tight by six hairgrips, as she hurled fish into the hot fat of the fryers.

'What a quaint custom,' mused the pelican. 'The fish is quite delicious raw. Still, I'm an adventurous bird. I'll have scampi for starters, followed by plaice if it's really fresh. Perhaps some halibut. There's always a place in my pouch for more.'

'How about a saveloy or a gherkin?' suggested Gerald, but the pelican shuddered in disgust.

It saw a jar of pickled eggs and muttered, 'Murderers!', but brightened up when it noticed a spare trilby and put it on. The trilby came down over its eyes and the pelican treated Gerald to a little dance routine. Then it said, 'Watch this.'

It sidled up to a woman ahead of them in the queue who had ordered haddock and chips seven times, and opened its beak wide. Distracted as she counted out her money, the woman dropped the seven little parcels one by one straight into the pelican's beak instead of her basket. Its pouch stretched and sagged right down to the floor.

'I can't take you anywhere,' said Gerald. He flung open the top of the pelican's beak just as you would open a flip-top bin, whipped out the seven lots of fish and dropped them into the woman's basket while she was still occupied with her money.

When they had bought food for all the campaigners, they wandered back to the playground. Gerald held the carrier of food in one hand and fed the pelican with the other, popping the pieces into its wide-open beak. After each piece it threw back its head and shook down the fish, swallowing loudly. When it belched and announced that it had had the fill of its bill for now, Gerald said, 'Tell me about the Riverside Massacre, pelican.'

It shuddered. 'Riverside,' it murmured. 'Every bird hears that word with horror. Since you ask, Gerald, I must tell you the whole painful story. Two years ago, fully-grown males of your species built a factory on the river bank not many miles from here. The river had been home to many generations of waterbirds – coots, mallards, mandarins, swans, dippers and kingfishers, to name a few. The river was rich in food and they lived there in harmony. At first, the birds took little notice of the factory.'

'What did they make there?' asked Gerald.

'They made clippers for trimming long hair that grows out of noses and ears, and special tweezers for pulling corns off toes. They made a lotion to make hair sprout out of bald heads, and cream to make necks look young instead of old and wrinkled. All things for people, of course, Gerald. Nothing for birds. Nothing for feather loss, receding webs or dry, scaly beaks,' grumbled the pelican.

Gerald giggled. 'Did these things work?' he asked. 'Did they get rid of the corns and wrinkles and make hair grow back?'

'Of course not,' said the pelican. 'Neither did the Lean Machine.'

'What was the Lean Machine?'

'It was a patented fat wobbler. It pummelled fat parts and made them thin. At least, it was supposed to make them thin, but a little bird told me it just gave them bruises. It cost hundreds of pounds. The people who owned the factory became very rich indeed.'

'What happened in the end?' asked Gerald, fearing that he knew the answer.

'They began to die,' said the pelican.

'Who?'

'The first was a duckling. Then

its brothers. Then five cygnets and their parents. One died long before the other. That was a tragedy. Some say the cob died of a broken heart after watching his children and his wife die.'

'Why did they die?' whispered Gerald.

'They were poisoned by the chemicals poured into the water from the factory. The whole river was poisoned, Gerald. Fish, weed and water creatures, and the birds who fed on them. That polluted water flowed on down to the estuary. We suspect there were deaths among geese and wading birds there. Your mother took up the cause, Gerald.'

'Yes I remember all the letters and phone calls when she came in every night from work. Dad said it was a pity she didn't take up cake-decorating or flouncing about dressed as a dusky maiden like old Mrs Jones in the local operatic society. He said at least we wouldn't have such a big phone bill. And I thought it was just about a lot of dirty water. I didn't realize it was so – so dreadful. What happened to the owners of the factory? Were they sent to prison?'

'Prison? On no. They had to pay a tiny fine and say they'd be good in the future. They have friends in high places. Your species say they have made lots of laws to protect their fellow creatures, Gerald. These just protect their consciences. When the chips are down, they always put their own species first.'

'Who were the owners?' asked Gerald.

'The Sneedies, of course. They were responsible for the Riverside Massacre,' said the pelican. 'And they'll be responsible for a lot more if we don't act fast. You know, Gerald, I have often pondered on the reasons for Romoana Sneedie's behaviour. Perhaps her egg was knocked around? A traumatic hatching maybe, or an unhappy chickhood? Yet when the chips are down – which I see yours are already, Gerald, from your empty chip-bag! – we cannot excuse her greed and her blindness to the needs of others.'

'It's a good job you're here,' said Gerald.

'I knew that the pond was under threat. I didn't realize the final confrontation would be so soon. Now then, Gerald, feed your mother and her flock. Then take them to the pond. I am weary. We sit in circles to fish, utterly still. It concentrates the mind wonderfully, and I feel the need for some meditation now.' It touched its wings together in front of its beak and then shuffled into the nearby doorway of the Bon Saucisse French Restaurant.

'That doesn't look like a very good place to meditate,' frowned Gerald, but the pelican stayed motionless, eyes closed, wingtips touching.

Only as Gerald hurried away did it open one marble eye. It struggled against the door of the restaurant and plummeted into the dark interior.

CHAPTER NINE

'Thanks, love,' said Gerald's mother when he handed her the food. Some of the protesters had gone. The toddlers in the buggies had been taken home for alphabetti spaghetti and sleep. The people who were still there fell upon the food as if they hadn't eaten for a week.

'Thanks for fetching this, Gerald,' said his mum. 'You were an awful long time. Was there a queue?'

'Er, yes,' said Gerald, truthfully. 'Now listen, Mum. Not only has Romoana Sneedie sold off the playground, but she's also planning to get rid of the park up the road too. The one with the pond. She's meeting the

Press there very soon.'

'How do you know, Gerald?' said his mum. 'Have you started to read the future in empty chip papers?'

'I KNOW!' cried Gerald. 'This is the last chance to stop our town becoming Sneedie City.'

His mother saw that he was serious. 'Right, come on, everyone!' she cried. 'The Sneedies are trying to get rid of the pond too.'

A roar of anger rose up. It was a very big roar from such a small band of people. Snatching up their belongings, the protesters hurried on down the High Street. They ran past a row of empty shops which had been boarded up. Looking at the vacant buildings now, they wondered if the shopkeepers had been driven out by Sneedie Enterprises.

The pond was in a small park next to the Nightcap and Ferret.

'I bet your dad is still in there playing darts,' said Gerald's mum. 'I bet his overtime is over. I hope he doesn't pin too many cheese sandwiches to the wall.'

'This park is a pleasant place,' said a man in the group called John. 'My auntie comes here every Thursday after Sainsbury's. Just look at those roses and sweet williams.'

The pond sat in the middle of the flowerbeds with a narrow path between them. Gerald saw mallards and coots on the water and a pair of pretty mandarins. On the path stood some large ducks which looked as if someone had stuck melted red balloons all round their beaks.

'They're Muscovy ducks,' said John.

'Why does she want this place?' puzzled Gerald's mother. 'The old people sit here in the sunshine and chat, and the children love to feed the birds. Look at that little girl.'

A child of two or three was tossing pieces of bread into the pond and crowing with delight as the ducks dabbled it and then gobbled it up. Gerald's mother started talking to the child's mother who said, 'Her biggest treat is to come to this park and feed the ducks. We've not even a garden or a goldfish at home.'

'What a charming scene,' gushed a familiar voice. 'So touching. Just think, you are all witnessing the very last time a child will feed these ducks on this pond. And this is the last time a mother will smile sweetly at the sight of her contented infant chucking crusts at those useless bundles of feathers. Ah well! That's progress for you.'

And there was ... Romoana Sneedie striking poses in front of the photographer from the local paper.

Nine shots later she announced, 'The caption for these photos will be, "First Lady Sneedie goes walkabout among the local yobbos — I mean, townsfolk. New future for the pond with Remarkable Romoana."'

The photographer nodded meekly and Gerald's mum snapped, 'Of course, the Sneedies practically own our local paper, so you'll have to print that, won't you?'

A reporter waved a notebook and called, 'Will the park and pond be kept for everyone? Will they just be under new management, Councillor?'

'Ah ha, wouldn't you like to know,' smirked Romoana. 'We may have other plans for them. More exciting plans.'

'What do you mean by "*we*"?' cried Gerald's mum. 'The people in this town are "we". We love to come here to see the ducks and smell the flowers. It's a peaceful haven from the busy High Street. And the pond is the only place for miles around to provide a habitat for wildlife. Especially since someone polluted the river. We need waterbirds!'

From nearby, Gerald thought he heard the sound of wings clapping.

Councillor Sneedie closed her eyes as if the thought of wildlife and waterbirds was quite ridiculous. She said, 'We have given waterbirds every chance, every opportunity. What do they do? They don't make any money. They just paddle around and make disgusting messes. They contribute nothing to the economy. As far as I'm concerned, the only useful duck is one cooked in orange sauce.'

'Outrageous!' came the squawk, and Gerald shouted, 'People need birds, Mrs Sneedie. The whole world needs birds. Why, some people at my school don't know what a mallard, coot or – or even a pelican, looks like. They don't know what they're missing!'

'Not you again, boy,' sneered Romoana. 'People don't need birds, they need freedom of choice. MY choice!'

'Well, the townspeople's choice is to keep that pond!' shouted Gerald's mum. 'You can't just take it from them.'

'Oh, can't I?' simpered Romoana Sneedie. 'I'm afraid I already have. And I have invited the constable here to witness my authorization before we proceed. Now where is he?'

'Here, Councillor,' gasped PC Smartish, hurrying back from his tea-break at the station (a mug of Earl Grey and six Jammy Dodgers). 'I'm here, three o'clock on the dot. I must say, I do hope you'll be nice to the dickybirds, Councillor.'

'Do you? I'm *so* sorry. You see, on behalf of the Council I have sold the playground *and* the park with the pond to a dear friend from Texas. He will build a hotel and leisure complex all along this High Street. There will be a casino, a lido and a wonderful steakhouse serving bits of Mr Greedyfeller's cattle from his Texas ranch. There will be no common riff-raff allowed. It will be exclusive, extensive, and extremely expensive. And I will share in the profits. Tee-hee!'

'What?' cried PC Smartish. 'Councillor Sneedie, I must ask you to show the authorization for this. I have to see the proof that this Mr Greedyfeller has really bought the land from the Council.'

'In a minute,' she said. 'But let me share my plans with you. The document is safely in my bag, and my flattening force is over there, all ready to flatten and fill before your very eyes! Look there!' She pointed, posing like the Statue of Liberty, her red bag held high instead of a torch.

As the crowd watched, horrified, two trucks roared into the car park at the back. They spun round and backed up towards the pond. They were dumper trucks. And they were full to the brim with things to dump.

Behind them chugged a shiny blue roadroller with a large satin bow still on the bonnet. Gerald recognized the lollipop shape of Norris Sneedie at the steering wheel.

'Mr I.M.A. Greedyfeller himself is in command of one dumper truck,' gushed Romoana. 'And my trusty chauffeur drives the other. One of the trucks is full of earth from a local beauty spot. The earth wasn't doing much at the beauty spot. It will be much more useful filling in this pond. And the other truck is slopping away with very wet cement to put a nice concrete surface on the earth. I'm sure we all know what my roadroller is there for! It doesn't only flatten tarmac.'

She put her head on one side and laughed. Her eyes bulged and reminded Gerald of those joke eyeballs that dangle down on springs. 'There's nothing anyone can do about it, I'm afraid,' she smiled.

'There's nothing any *person* can do, but what about a pelican?' muttered Gerald. 'Where is the wretched bird?'

'Councillor – I repeat, I must see your authorization, your bill of sale,' said PC Smartish.

'Certainly, Officer,' beamed Romoana. She took the rolled-up document from the bag and said, 'Perhaps you would like to read it out to us all, Mrs Do-Gooder?'

Gerald's mum took the paper. She unrolled it slowly. She stared at it. She sighed.

'Every Council member has signed this,' she said sadly. Then she read: '"On this fourteenth day of March, the High Street children's playground and the park containing a pond have been sold on the Council's behalf to – to . . ."'

Gerald waited with baited breath.

Romoana said teasingly, 'Come on,

let's hear it. Sold to—?'

'"A. Crested Pelican Esquire!"' read out Gerald's mum. '"Being the Perchbird of, and acting on behalf of, the Waterbirds' Ponds and Pools Committee." Who's he when he's at home?'

'Who indeed!' smirked Gerald, watching Romoana Sneedie's face turn the colour of tapioca pudding.

'Utter nonsense!' she shrieked. 'Give me that!'

But PC Smartish had taken control of the situation and the piece of paper.

'She's right, Councillor,' he said. 'There's no mention of any Mr Greedyfeller. He must have been a figment of your imagination. There's a great big waterbird's footprint here, like a signature. A web of intrigue, you might say.'

But Romoana Sneedie was not amused. 'How much has this – this Mr Crested Pelican paid for the land?' she spluttered. 'Did he put in a higher bid after ours?'

'Well now, let me see,' smiled Gerald's mum. 'It says, "Bought for the sum of a pouchful of fish soup."'

'That is ridiculous!' screeched Romoana.

'On the contrary, my dear madam, it is a very reasonable price,' came the authoritative squawk. 'On behalf of the Council, please accept payment by direct debit from my pouch with the compliments of the world's waterbirds.'

The pelican hovered above her head like an avenging angel. It jack-knifed so that it was upside down and then disgorged from its pillowcase pouch a rancid mess of brown liquid, slimy onions, bones and fish, which was definitely rotten, all over Romoana.

'So that's why you went into the Bon Saucisse,' said Gerald.

'This is last month's bouillabaisse, Gerald,' it said. 'I did sample one or two items from their *poissons à la carte* first. Naturally.' It flapped over the dripping head of rancid

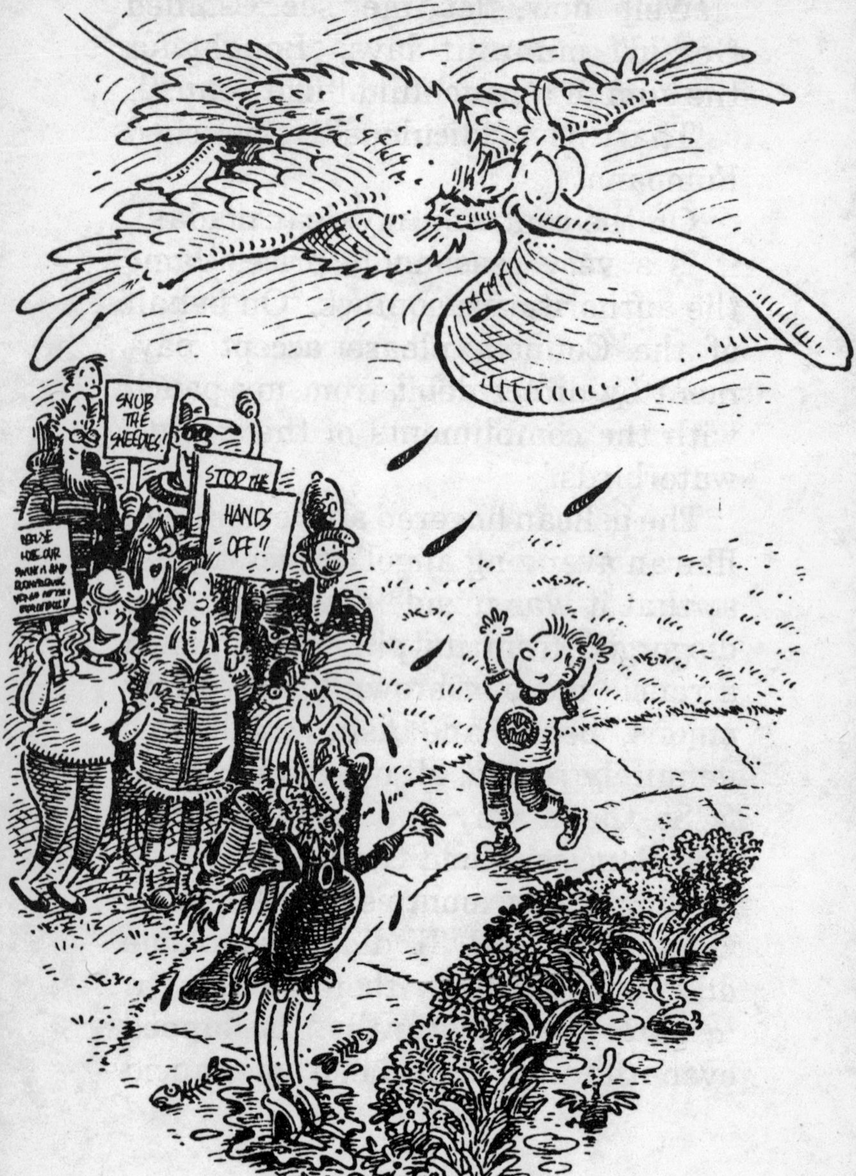
SNUB THE SNEEDIES!
STOP THE
HANDS OFF!!

Romoana and squawked, 'Freedom for the freshwater brothers! Birds of the world unite and fight,' over its shoulder at a couple of fascinated sparrows.

'Well,' said PC Smartish, rocking to and fro on his heels as he'd seen the police do in old films. 'It's all signed, sealed and delivered. Reclaimed on behalf of the dickybirds.'

'Hurray!' shouted everyone. 'Hurray!'

But they shouted too soon.

Romoana Sneedie turned towards the trucks, her wet hair wild as a scarecrow's head of cornstalks adorned with a fish tail. Her suit was spattered with onions and the bow at her collar dripped brownly. She stank.

Yet Romoana Sneedie just couldn't bear to lose. She snapped her fingers and shouted, 'DUMPER TRUCKS ROLL!'

And all the little birds on the pond hid their heads under their wings.

CHAPTER TEN

The truck full of the local beauty spot began to raise its load slowly, oh so slowly, ready to tip it into the pond.

Gerald heard his mother say, 'There's nothing else for it now,' and saw her run towards the truck.

'Now what is she up to?' he groaned. 'Oh no! Not the teachings of Gandhi Guillemot!' For his mother lay down by the edge of the pool, exactly where the earth would be dumped.

'Stop, stop!' shouted PC Smartish, and gabbled into his radio.

'Mum, Mum, who'll make my banana-and-peanut-butter sarnies if you get splatted on by the dumper truck?' shouted Gerald, running after PC Smartish, who was hurrying towards the cab of the dumper truck.

Someone beat him to it.

'Oi!' roared the someone. 'All right, so it's closing time. I don't need a poltergeist to get me out!'

From the doors of the Nightcap and Ferret charged Gerald's dad, darts still clutched in his hand and the pelican flapping round his head in a blizzard of feathers.

He dashed over to the lorry and Gerald saw him stabbing away at it with the darts, roaring, 'Take that! And that, you dirty rotten dumper!'

'I'll be an orphan,' Gerald sobbed inwardly. 'My mum will be dumped upon, and my dad will be inside for murder.'

The truck stopped.

Gerald's mum lifted up her head and grinned at Gerald's dad.

'Get up, Jean,' he said. 'Ooh, you do put me through it, love. First I hear these snotty Sneedies are buying up me local, and then I see them threatening my Jean with a lorry-load of earth. So I let their hydraulic fluid out with me darts. Makes up for losing the match.'

Gerald's mum got up and shouted, 'Do you accept defeat now, Mrs Sneedie?'

'Never!' screeched Romoana, wobbling away on her stiletto heels towards the other truck.

'Dump the cement, Irvin. Come on, man, DUMP THE CEMENT!'

He did as he was told, of course.

There was a moment's silence. Then the photographer began clicking and whirring away in excitement, and Gerald's dad said, 'She makes a nice new statue for the park, doesn't she?'

Romoana Sneedie was covered from head to handbag to high heels with wet cement. Only her eyes and mouth still showed through. And those eyes bulged with such fury that Gerald thought they might finally plop right out of her head and dangle there, still rolling.

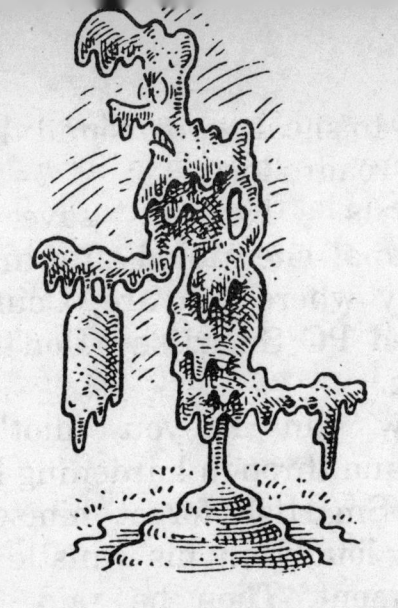

A tall figure lowered itself from the cab of the dumper lorry and drawled, 'Gee, Romoana. I knew you were a hard woman, but this is ridiculous. I guess we won't be doing business together again.'

'Too right, mate,' snapped a big sergeant, jumping out of a police car. 'You won't be doing any business with anybody. And neither will you, littl'un,' he said to the lollipop-shaped figure of Norris Sneedie, who was trying to sneak away round the back of the roadroller.

'Norris, Norris, save your Romoana!' she wailed after him.

'Stay where you are, Councillor,' ordered PC Smartish. 'Don't try to escape.'

'How can I, you idiot!' spat Romoana through hardening lips.

PC Smartish forgot himself and tooted loudly on his whistle in the excitement. Then he said, 'I'll be charging all three of you with attempted vandalism, and deceit and maybe fraud and – and – ooh, lots of things. I'll have to get Sarge to help me out. Let me warn you that anything you say may be taken down and used in evidence against you. Go on, don't be a spoilsport. Say something.'

Romoana Sneedie said not one word. Her lips were sealed.

PC Smartish sighed, then brightened up. 'I can send for the fire brigade to chip her out,' he said. 'That's novel, isn't it?'

'Yes,' laughed Gerald's mum. 'And I'll tell you what else is novel. That fish soup still stinks even though she's covered in cement.'

Gerald smiled and watched the pelican as it waddled over to the pond. When it reached the edge it stood on one leg like a big-footed ballet dancer in a tatty grey tutu. It stretched out its neck and raised one wing. The ducks on the pond came out and did the same. They were watching the sky as if they were waiting for something.

Tiny specks appeared high above, flying in formation.

'It's the Red Arrows,' said Gerald, but the sound wasn't right. He heard the beat of wings and saw them clearly now, flying in a 'V' formation – geese and gannets, cormorants and herons, petrels and pelicans. A crack squadron of waterbirds. There was an extraordinary music – an ocean symphony of cries, hissings, squawks and wing-beats. The pond birds were echoing the music from the ground, their heads craned upwards.

Gerald remembered the pelican telling him, 'We have other forms of communication,' and felt his head fill with the music.

The squadron of birds, sixty or more, flew low over the park. Every single bird banked and turned.

The pelican stood with his wing stretched to touch his crest in salute. He stayed motionless long after the majestic waterbird flypast had vanished beyond the clouds.

CHAPTER ELEVEN

The pelican was back at the house before Gerald and his parents arrived. It was in his bedroom, fast asleep on his bean-bag. Its head was swivelled back between its wings. Its eyes were covered by a filmy sort of eyelid and its beak was open. Every few seconds a snore rumbled deep in its pouch.

Gerald couldn't see any nostrils. Good job, too, he thought. Its fishy smell really was strong, although Gerald was getting used to it. In fact, he was getting used to the pelican altogether. He thought of it flying out of his life again and was sad. The big, ungainly, pompous bird was his friend. He loved it in a funny sort of way.

He ran down to the kitchen and opened a tin of tuna. He put a packet of fish fingers to defrost. The pelican would be hungry when it woke up.

He ran upstairs again. The pelican was still asleep. Gerald bent down and whispered under the fringe of feathers where he thought its ear might be, 'Here's some tuna. There'll be fish fingers soon, and I'm going for a bath. Then I'll read you *Treasure Island*.'

The pelican's eyes snapped open. 'Tip the tuna in, please,' it squawked. Then it waddled after Gerald into the bathroom and sang to itself while he bathed. 'I must say, this is all so fascinating, Gerald,' it said. 'What is in that bottle on the shelf?'

'It's called bath gel.'

'Oh, I suppose you use that as you haven't any feather oil. It's a shame for you all. And fancy having a cuttlefish bone. Good for the maintenance of one's beak, Gerald,' it said, popping something into its mouth from the side of the bath.

'That's not a cuttlefish bone – it's soap!' cried Gerald, as the pelican began to foam at the beak. 'Do you want some toothpaste to take the taste away?'

'I'd rather have an anchovy,' it said. 'Forgive me if I don't join you in the bath, Gerald, but all that bubble-bath detergent might spoil the natural balance of my feathers. They have felt a little harsh since this morning's dip into the washing-up water.'

'Was it only this morning?' said Gerald sadly. 'It seems ages ago.'

The pelican asked about the razor on the shelf. It chuckled in disbelief when Gerald explained.

'You mean the one with the big external ears shaves the feathers from his face, Gerald?' it cackled. 'You people are so entertaining!'

After the bath, Gerald read aloud to the pelican while it toyed with the fish fingers. Every time Gerald read a bit about Captain Flint, the parrot, the pelican clapped its webs together and squawked, 'Keep your pecker up, Captain Flint. It's good to see a bird in a book, Gerald. It raises the tone. Mind you,' it confided, 'Captain Flint was no waterbird, you know. He was a common ship's parrot. Quite unsophisticated. He couldn't catch a fish to save his life. And his feet were the primitive kind without any webs. Can you believe it, Gerald?'

Gerald finished *Treasure Island* that night. He had never, ever read aloud for so long. But it was the first pelican audience he had ever had.

He put down the book and crawled under his duvet. He felt very tired indeed and sad at having to say goodbye.

The pelican flipped off the light

switch with the tip of its wing. It said in its small gruff voice, 'The window is already open, Gerald. I must fly. I shall see you on the nineteenth.'

'The nineteenth?' whispered Gerald.

'That's what I said. Please pay attention, Gerald. I am fitting you into my schedule as we arranged. Every third Saturday. I wish to continue my studies of the human being in its natural habitat. And, of course, I shall continue in my duties as environmental activist for the waterbirds. I am sure your species will give me plenty to do.'

'If you say so, pelican,' murmured Gerald.

The ghostly shape of the big bird glimmered in the dusk. Gerald caught the gleam of its eye and, as he drifted away to sleep, he heard again that strange music of the wind and the ocean.

When Gerald woke up on Sunday

morning there was no pelican. Only a soft grey feather lay beside him on the pillow.

THE END

ATTILA THE HEN
by Paddy Mounter

'YOU, ATTILA THE HEN, HAVE BEEN SENT TO LEAD US TO FREEDOM!'

Being cooped up on a dirty, smelly battery farm is no life for any hen – least of all one as big and stroppy as Attila! She has *no* intention of ending up as chicken soup, and wastes no time in laying the plans for a daring escape – for herself and all her sisters.

Things don't go *eggzactly* as planned though, and Atilla and her band of intrepid chickens must dice with danger before finally coming home to roost!

A very funny adventure, starring an original and indomitable heroine – Attila the Hen.

0 440 86264 7

A SELECTED LIST OF TITLES AVAILABLE FROM YEARLING BOOKS

THE PRICES SHOWN BELOW WERE CORRECT AT THE TIME OF GOING TO PRESS. HOWEVER TRANSWORLD PUBLISHERS RESERVE THE RIGHT TO SHOW NEW RETAIL PRICES ON COVERS WHICH MAY DIFFER FROM THOSE PREVIOUSLY ADVERTISED IN THE TEXT OR ELSEWHERE.

☐ 86273 6 **STAYING NINE** Pam Conrad £2.50
☐ 86277 9 **SHRUBBERY SKULDUGGERY** Rebecca Lisle £2.50
☐ 86290 6 **TOM'S SAUSAGE LION** Michael Morpurgo £2.50
☐ 86264 7 **ATTILA THE HEN** Paddy Mounter £2.99
☐ 86265 5 **POOR BADGER** K. M. Peyton £2.50
☐ 86281 7 **KNOCKING JACK** Susan Price £2.99
☐ 86227 2 **ROOM 13** Robert Swindells £2.99
☐ 86275 2 **THE POSTBOX MYSTERY** Robert Swindells £2.50
☐ 86231 0 **GLUBBSLYME** Jacqueline Wilson £2.99
☐ 86279 5 **THE STORY OF TRACY BEAKER**
Jacqueline Wilson £2.50

All Yearling Books are available at your bookshop or newsagent, or can be ordered from the following address:
Transworld Publishers Ltd
Cash Sales Department
P.O. Box 11, Falmouth, Cornwall TR10 9EN

UK and B.F.P.O. customers please send a cheque or postal order (no currency) and allow £1.00 for postage and packing for the first book plus 50p for the second book and 30p for each additional book to a maximum charge of £3.00 (7 books plus).

Overseas customers, including Eire, please allow £2.00 for postage and packing for the first book plus £1.00 for the second book and 50p for each subsequent title ordered.

NAME (Block letters) ....

ADDRESS ....